First published by Parragon in 2012

Parragon
Chartist House
15–17 Trim Street
Bath BA1 1HA, UK
www.parragon.com

Edited by Sarah Mellowes
Designed by Pete Hampshire
Production by Emma Fulleylove

ISBN 978-1-4454-9652-8

Printed in China

Bath · New York · Singapore · Hong Kong · Cologne · Delhi
Melbourne · Amsterdam · Johannesburg · Shenzhen

Wreck-It Ralph lived in the *Fix-It Felix, Jr* video game.
The big-fisted Ralph was the Bad Guy, and Felix was the Good
Guy. Every time someone in the arcade played the game, Ralph
would yell, **"I'M GONNA WRECK IT!"**

As Ralph wrecked the apartment building, the Nicelanders
called for Felix's help, shouting **"FIX IT, FELIX!"**

Felix was always ready to fix anything with his magic hammer, and each time he did, the Nicelanders would give him a big shiny medal and a tasty pie.

Ralph, however, would get thrown off the top of the building, into a mud puddle below.

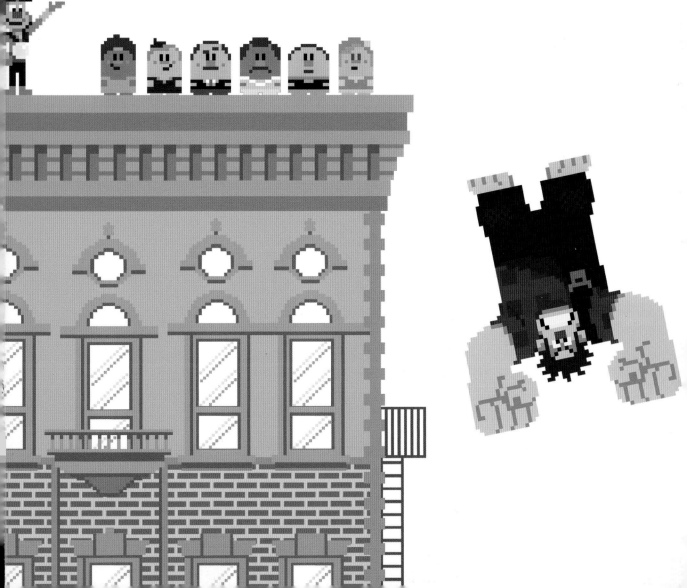

The *Fix-It Felix, Jr* game was one of the older games in the arcade, and had been in Litwak's Family Fun Centre for thirty years now. With all the new, high-tech games, the original 8-bit game was still a favourite with the kids.

But thirty years of being thrown in the mud made Ralph feel sad. It just wasn't fair.

One night, Ralph attended a support group for video game Bad Guys. He told the group how unhappy he was at always being the Bad Guy.

"We can't change who we are," the others said. Then they all recited the Bad Guy Affirmation: "I am Bad. And that's good. I will never be Good. And that's not bad. There's no one I'd rather be than me."

That evening, the Nicelanders held a thirtieth-anniversary party. Ralph couldn't believe that he hadn't been invited. Wasn't he a big part of the game, too?

"I am going to that party!" Ralph decided.

Felix let Ralph join the party. When the cake arrived, Ralph saw a tiny Felix figurine on the top wearing a medal. Then he spotted the candy version of himself, in a chocolate mud puddle. Ralph wanted to be the one wearing a medal!

"Bad Guys don't win medals!" Nicelander Gene said angrily.

Ralph was so upset that he accidentally **wrecked the cake**!
Ralph looked at the Nicelanders. They were all upset and covered in frosting. Feeling sad, Ralph left, alone.

Ralph travelled into a neighbouring game for a root beer. A soldier named Private Markowski staggered in. He had come from a new first-person shooter game called *Hero's Duty*, where the goal was to battle swarms of cy-bugs and climb a tower to win the **Medal of Heroes**.

A small bug suddenly scuttled across the table and Markowski fainted. Ralph decided to borrow Markowski's armour and **find that medal!**

Ralph sneaked into *Hero's Duty*. But as soon as the game started, ʜᴜɴɢʀʏ ᴄʏ-ʙᴜɢꜱ began to attack, gobbling up characters, vehicles and weapons! Then they turned into whatever they ate.

Ralph was terrified! He fled, as a voice suddenly boomed, "ɢᴀᴍᴇ ᴏᴠᴇʀ!"

The *Hero's Duty* game began to reset. A beacon appeared
at the top of the tower, and the cy-bugs immediately flew
into the light, which ZAPPED them one by one.

Sergeant Calhoun, the soldiers' leader, was furious
that Ralph hadn't followed the game's rules properly.
But Ralph wasn't listening. He was thinking about how
to get the Medal of Heroes from the top of the tower!

In the arcade, one of the kids dropped her coin into *Fix-It Felix, Jr*, but Ralph didn't show up to wreck the apartment building. Felix had nothing to fix!

"Mr Litwak!" the girl called out. **"This game's busted!"**

Inside the game, the Nicelanders were worried. Mr Litwak had just put an 'OUT OF ORDER' sign on the screen. If Ralph didn't return, the game would be unplugged forever!

Felix knew he had to find Ralph and bring him back.

"I can fix this!" Felix said to his fellow Nicelanders, and off he went.

Inside *Hero's Duty*, Ralph had climbed
his way to the top of the tower.
He carefully tiptoed through lots of
cy-bug eggs to reach the Medal of Heroes.
Finally, he had a medal of his own!

Suddenly, Ralph knocked over a cy-bug egg. The egg cracked open and a baby cy-bug hurled itself onto Ralph's face! He fell into an escape pod, which launched into the sky. The escape pod rocketed down a tunnel towards Game Central Station, the hub for all of the arcade games.

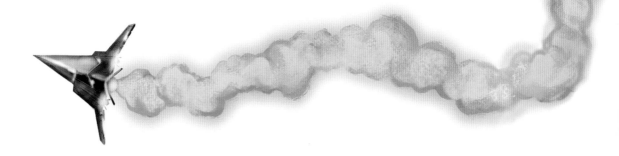

The pod zoomed through Game Central and crash-landed inside a colourful, sweet-looking world. Ralph was ejected from the pod and the cy-bug finally disappeared, sinking into a bubbling pool of toffee.

Ralph was confused. Then he realized he was in a video game called *SUGAR RUSH*.

"*Sugar Rush?*" he moaned. "Oh, man, this is that candy go-kart game!"

Ralph knew he had to get out of there before the arcade reopened. But where was his medal? *IT HAD VANISHED!*

Ralph spotted his Medal of Heroes hanging in a peppermint tree. He tried to grab it, but a little girl named Vanellope got to the medal first. She thought it was a gold coin.

"RACE YOU FOR IT!" she replied.

Poor Ralph just wanted his medal back. But as soon as he reached for another branch, he fell straight into a gooey toffee swamp.

At the *Sugar Rush* stadium, the **RANDOM ROSTER RACE** was about to begin. King Candy explained that each racer needed a gold coin to enter. The top finishers would appear as game characters the next day.

Vanellope stepped out of the shadows, pushing her rickety little kart. *CLANG!* She threw Ralph's medal into the pot ... and her name appeared on the list of racers!

The crowd gasped in shock. To them, Vanellope was a *GLITCH* – a mistake in the game's programming. She wasn't supposed to race! Quickly, King Candy ordered the Donut Police to take her away.

Just then, Ralph smashed his way onto the track, desperate to get his medal back.

"*THIEF!*" he cried at Vanellope, and ran after her, wrecking everything in his path as he did so.

Ralph was taken to King Candy's castle. The king told Ralph that the medal would go to the winner of the next race.

King Candy ordered Ralph to leave *Sugar Rush*, but Ralph wouldn't leave without his medal! Then ... *CRASH*! Ralph smashed his way through the castle wall and escaped!

Ralph tracked Vanellope through the Lollistix
Forest, but a group of other racers had just arrived.
They demanded Vanellope drop out of the race,
then they smashed her kart and *TOSSED HER INTO
A CHOCOLATE PUDDLE.*

This made Ralph **_VERY ANGRY_**! He chased
the racers away.

Ralph told Vanellope he'd never be able to
get another medal. She suddenly had an idea.

"You help me build a kart and then I'll win
you back your medal. It's a classic win-win."

Reluctantly, Ralph agreed to help her.

In another part of *Sugar Rush*, Felix and Calhoun found the wrecked escape pod, but there was no sign of Ralph — or the cy-bug. Calhoun asked Felix why Ralph would want to leave his own game.

"I never thought he'd *GO TURBO*," Felix said, worriedly.

"Go Turbo?" asked Calhoun.

Then Felix told Calhoun the story of Turbo – a popular character who was a star until a new racing game arrived at the arcade.

Turbo was so jealous that he *SNEAKED INTO THE NEW GAME*.

But when Turbo appeared in the wrong game, everyone thought it was broken! The games became glitchy, so Mr Litwak had them both unplugged and hauled away.

"I can't let that happen to my game," said Felix.

Elsewhere, Vanellope and Ralph sneaked into the *Sugar Rush* kart bakery to bake a new kart. *SPLAT! WHOOSH!* They spilled and splattered ingredients everywhere!

Ralph looked at the finished kart and sighed.

"Kid ... I tried to warn you, I don't make things, I ... "

"I love it. I love it. *I LOVE IT!*" Vanellope replied, delighted.

Just then, King Candy arrived with his security force. Ralph threw Vanellope into the driver's seat.

"I DON'T KNOW HOW TO DRIVE!" Vanellope cried.

Ralph had to steer the kart himself, as Vanellope directed him to her hideaway inside Diet Cola Mountain. A huge stalactite of Mentos candy hung over a hot spring of diet cola.

To get his medal back, Ralph knew that he had to help Vanellope win that race. He wrecked the rocks around the lake to create a racetrack for Vanellope to practise.

Soon, she was zooming along.
She was a natural!
Perhaps Vanellope *could* win
... as long as she could keep her
GLITCHING and ***TWITCHING***
under control!

Just before Vanellope and Ralph left for the race, King Candy found Ralph alone. He told Ralph that Vanellope didn't belong in the game — if players in the arcade saw her glitching, *Sugar Rush* would be doomed.

He gave the medal over and asked Ralph to stop Vanellope racing, in order to protect her.

Moments later, Vanellope arrived with a homemade medal for Ralph. It said 'YOU'RE MY HERO'.

"I made it for you, in case we don't win," said Vanellope.

Ralph felt terrible. He knew he was about to crush her dreams.

Then, Vanellope spotted the
Medal of Heroes in Ralph's pocket.
"You sold me out?" asked
Vanellope, feeling betrayed.
"You're a rat! And I don't need
you! I can win the race on my own!"
She started to wail.

Ralph tried to tell Vanellope that she would confuse the players, and because she was a glitch, she couldn't leave her game. But Vanellope wouldn't listen, so Ralph **WRECKED HER KART**!

"You really are a Bad Guy!" Vanellope shrieked. Ralph picked up his Medal of Heroes and walked sadly away.

Sad and alone, Ralph returned to the *Fix-It Felix, Jr* game. The Nicelanders had fled, worried the game would be scrapped. As he hurled his medal away, it hit the game's front screen and the 'OUT OF ORDER' sign slipped. Suddenly, he could see the *Sugar Rush* game with Vanellope's picture on it. She *did* belong in *Sugar Rush*!

Ralph needed some answers. He hurried back to *Sugar Rush* and spotted King Candy's sidekick, Sour Bill, cleaning up Vanellope's kart.

Sour Bill revealed the truth: Vanellope was a real racer in the game, and King Candy had stolen her computer code. If she ever crossed the finish line, she would be fully restored to the game!

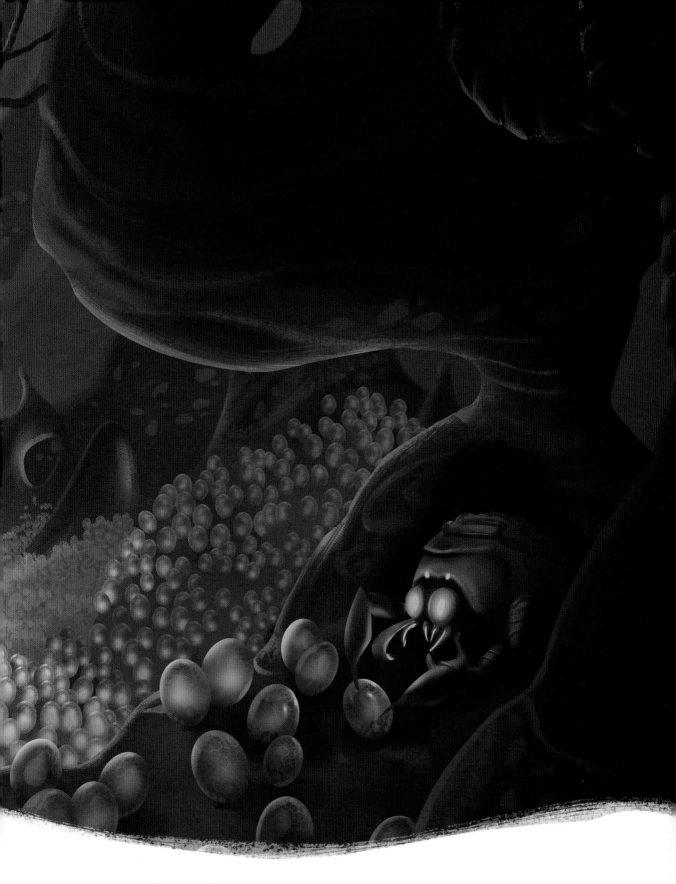

Meanwhile, Calhoun had travelled across *Sugar Rush* and
was scanning for cy-bugs. Suddenly, she fell into a giant
cavern that was riddled with cy-bugs. The original cy-bug
had multiplied! Calhoun had to act quickly, otherwise the
whole arcade would be *DOOMED*!

Ralph had to get Vanellope back in the race. Learning that both Felix and Vanellope were locked up in King Candy's dungeon, he **WRECKED** his way through the castle walls, firstly into Felix's cell.

Then ... *BAM*! Ralph crashed through
to Vanellope's cell.
  "I know, I know," Ralph told her.
"I'm an idiot."
  "And?" she asked.
  "And a stink brain?" he replied.
Vanellope beamed. "The stinkiest brain ever!"
  At last, they were a team again!

Ralph, Vanellope and Felix rushed to the stadium, and Ralph pushed her onto the track. The Donut Police couldn't stop her this time!

Vanellope quickly glitched past the other racers, and she soon caught up with King Candy.

"This is my kingdom!" snarled King Candy.

RACE YOU FOR IT! Vanellope replied.

King Candy slammed into Vanellope's kart. She concentrated very hard ... and glitched away just in time. Then King Candy glitched, too!

The crowd gasped as they watched the race on the big screen. King Candy's glitching revealed his true identity – he was *TURBO*!

"You've ruined everything!" Turbo screamed at Vanellope.

Vanellope zoomed ahead – she was in the lead!

"You're going to do it!" Ralph cheered from up inside King Candy's box, as Vanellope raced towards the finish line.

Just then, disaster struck – swarms of cy-bugs burst out from under the racetrack, destroying it completely. *THEY HAD MULTIPLIED*, and one of them gobbled up King Candy!

Ralph grabbed Vanellope just in time.
The crowd ran for the tunnel to Game Central
Station, but Vanellope was a glitch so couldn't
leave the game. There was no way Ralph would
leave without her!

It's Minty! Cool

Calhoun arrived to fight the cy-bugs, but Ralph realized they needed a beacon of light to draw the bugs away. Ralph had an idea ... he would create his own beacon! He climbed up Diet Cola Mountain and started to **SMASH** his way through the top of the crater. Suddenly, the same cy-bug that ate Turbo began to attack him!

"I've got you now, Bad Guy!" the King Candy-bug shouted.

The evil King Candy-bug lifted Ralph into the air. Ralph escaped the King Candy-bug's grip, and fell, crashing down into the candy crater. The Mentos stalactite broke loose and fell into the hot diet cola below, along with Ralph. Suddenly, someone glitched through the mountain and grabbed him just in time. *IT WAS VANELLOPE!*

But then ... *KABOOM*! The Mentos stalactite broke loose and crashed into the hot diet cola spring. A glowing fountain spewed out of the mountaintop. At once, all the cy-bugs in the whole of *Sugar Rush* turned and flew straight into the bright light. Not even the King Candy-bug could resist.

ZAP-ZAP! All of them were destroyed one by one, just as they had been in *Hero's Duty*.

Felix got to work fixing the finish line. Then Ralph pushed Vanellope across it. The computer recognized her code immediately, and suddenly Vanellope turned into a *PRINCESS*!

At last, everyone knew the truth. King Candy had stolen Vanellope's royal identity, and now she had it back. Vanellope wasn't keen on being a princess though — she just wanted to carry on racing!

"Glitching is my super power. I'm not giving that up," she told Ralph, happily.

The arcade was due to open any minute, so everyone needed to return to their games. Vanellope gave Ralph a huge hug.

"You could just stay here and live in the castle. You could be happy," she said.

"I'm already happy," replied Ralph, "*BECAUSE I HAVE THE COOLEST FRIEND IN THE WORLD.*"

Felix rushed Ralph back to the *Fix-It Felix, Jr* game.

As Ralph and Felix raced back to *Fix-It Felix, Jr*, Mr Litwak was about to unplug the power cord. Just in time, Ralph appeared on the screen and yelled, **"I'M GONNA WRECK IT!"** Mr Litwak couldn't believe it! Ralph started to wreck the Nicelanders' apartment building. **The game was saved!**

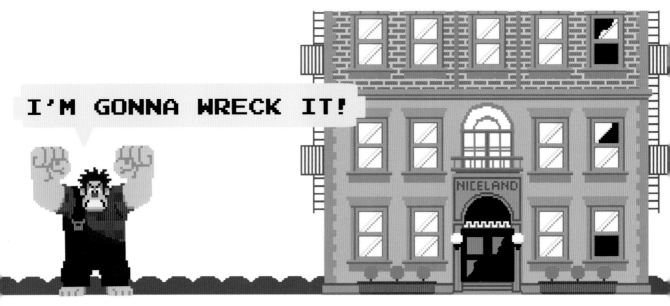

From then on, everyone in the game became friends. Ralph
didn't mind being thrown from the top of the building anymore,
and, from up high, he could see Vanellope happily racing
through *Sugar Rush*. She was really good!

Ralph finally realized that he didn't need a medal to prove he was good. He would always work as a Bad Guy, wrecking everything in sight, but now he had friends.

Best of all, he knew Vanellope was happy. And if he could make a little girl like her happy, how bad could he be?